PADDINGTON GOES SHOPPING

Paddington Picture Book 4

For older children Michael Bond has
written nine Paddington story books,
all illustrated by Peggy Fortnum

Text © Copyright Michael Bond 1973
Illustrations © Copyright Fred Banbery 1973
First published 1973

ISBN 0 00 182114 8

Made and Printed in Great Britain by
William Collins Sons & Co Ltd Glasgow

Paddington Goes Shopping

MICHAEL BOND AND FRED BANBERY

COLLINS
ST JAMES'S PLACE, LONDON

One day, not long after Paddington went to live
with the Browns at number thirty-two Windsor
Gardens, Mrs Brown thought she would take
him out shopping.

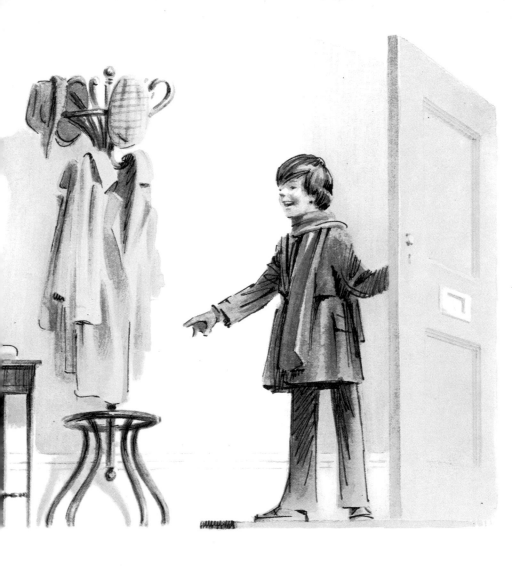

"We're going to the Portobello Road," explained Judy. "It's a big market quite near here."

"I should bring your pocket money," added Jonathan. "There's a lot to see."

Paddington didn't need asking twice and soon
afterwards they all set off.

Suddenly they turned a corner and he found
himself in what seemed like a different world: a

world of shops and street barrows, gold and silver ornaments, books, old furniture, fruit and vegetables, people . . . his eyes grew larger and larger as he tried to take it all in.

One shop was even having its photograph taken.
"That's a new supermarket," explained Judy.
"There must be something special on."
Paddington's mouth began to water as he

peered through the glass. "Perhaps I could do
some shopping for you, Mrs Brown?" he said
hopefully.

Mrs Brown hesitated. She wasn't at all sure about letting him go off on his own quite so soon, but Jonathan told her not to worry.

"Even Paddington can't get lost in a supermarket," he said. "What goes in must come out."

"We can meet him by the cash desk on our
way back," added Judy.

Paddington felt most important as he entered the shop.

He lifted his hat to the manager, who was standing just inside the door, and then consulted Mrs Brown's shopping list.

Everywhere he looked there were shelves
piled high with packets and tins. There was
even one shelf with nothing but marmalade,
so he could quite see why it was called
a *super*market.

His paws were soon full and he was just
beginning to wish he'd left his suitcase at home
when he saw the manager coming towards him
pushing a large basket on wheels.

"May I suggest you have one of these, sir?"
he called.

"You can take as much as you want now," he
continued.

"Can I really?" exclaimed Paddington.

The manager nodded. "Yes, we like to make

our customers happy.''

Paddington looked most impressed. ''In that case,'' he said, ''I think I'll have *two* baskets – just to make sure.''

The more Paddington saw of the supermarket the more he liked it, and he felt sure Mrs Brown would be pleased when she saw all her free groceries.

The other customers looked on in amazement.
"Perhaps he's trying to win an eating prize,"
suggested one lady, as he went past, his baskets
laden with goods.

But the customers weren't the only ones who
were watching Paddington with interest.

Since he had been in the shop the manager had
been joined by several other important looking
men, and as he reached the cash desk one of
them gave a signal, and they all started to clap.

Paddington had never been in a shop where
they tried so hard to make their customers
happy, and he gave the men a friendly wave as
he unloaded his baskets.

"Well done!" said the lady, handing him a
ticket. "I hope you've brought a lorry with you.
There's over fifty pounds' worth here!"

Paddington stared at the long roll of paper in his paw.

"*Over fifty pounds' worth*!" he gasped, hardly able to believe his eyes or his ears.

Giving the man who had said he could take as much as he wanted one of his hardest ever stares, he opened his suitcase and peered inside.

"But I've only got threepence!"

Looking up, Paddington suddenly caught sight
of a crowd of people coming towards him.

"Watch out!" cried the lady as he made a
grab for his shopping.

But it was too late. With a roar like an express
train the whole lot began to tumble down off the
counter.

Paddington was still sitting on the floor covered
with groceries when the Browns rushed into the
shop to see what was going on.

All in all he decided he was much safer where
he was for the time being.

"You wouldn't think," said the manager, "that giving someone a prize would be so difficult."

"A *prize*?" echoed the Browns. The manager pointed to a large notice on the wall.

"This young bear," he said, "happens to be our thousandth customer today.

Perhaps you'd like to tell him he's won a free supply of groceries!"

"All of which," said Judy, as they staggered home laden with shopping, "only goes to show that bears always fall on their feet."

"Even in supermarkets!" agreed Jonathan.

Paddington sniffed the air happily. "I like the Portobello Road," he said. "I think I shall always do my shopping here from now on."